WAKE UP, BEAR... IT'S CHRISTMAS!

Stephen Gammell

HEINEMANN : LONDON

William Heinemann Ltd
10 Upper Grosvenor Street, London W1X 9PA
LONDON MELBOURNE AUCKLAND JOHANNESBURG

First published in Great Britain 1982
Reprinted 1986
Copyright © 1981 by Stephen Gammell
SBN 434 94010 0

Filmset in Century Textbook by
Reproduction Drawings Ltd., Sutton, Surrey
Printed and bound in Hong Kong

To Jason, Nancy, and Janet

As the last few leaves of autumn fell, Bear was padding down his walking trail. He was going home for his winter's sleep. But he wasn't going to be sleeping all winter.

"That's right," he said, as he reached his door.
"I've missed it now for seven years,
and seems I've heard it said
that it's a happy, joyful time,
but always I'm in bed.
Well, this year things are different.
I've decided what to do.
I'm getting up for Christmas,
instead of sleeping through!"

After setting his clock and fixing his bed, Bear blew out the candle. Feeling happy but tired, he snuggled down under his blanket.

"Well," he yawned, "when I wake up
I wonder what I'll see.
Anyway, I hope it's fun
when Christmas comes to . . ."

He fell asleep.

The weeks went by. The forest was still and silent. The only sound was the wind as it blew softly during the day, and harder at night.

The snow started to fall late one afternoon. It fell gently at first, then became heavier. Soon, snow covered nearly everything in the forest. It almost came up to Bear's window.

Bear slept.

The clock woke him late one wintry afternoon. Sitting up slowly, Bear rubbed his eyes. Then he remembered it was Christmas Eve! His nose was cold as he smelled the fresh snow.

Putting on his scarf and mittens, he went out into the woods, where he found a nice little pine tree.

Back home in the candlelight, he
decorated his tree.

He got an old stocking from his cupboard, and hung it up by his window. Then humming a little tune, Bear fixed his blanket and sat back with his guitar to enjoy the evening.

"There. Everything looks cosy now,
and festive, I believe.
I'm so glad I'm wide awake
tonight on Christmas Eve."

He had not been sitting long when he heard a tapping sound at his door. Just a branch in the winter wind, he thought. But then he heard it again. It was a knock. Before Bear could move, the door opened.

"Hello, Bear. I saw your light.
I'll warm myself, if that's all right?"

Delighted by this unexpected visitor, Bear got up and invited him in.

"Well, hello stranger, come on in.
Don't stand out there and freeze.
It's warm inside and you can rest—
here, take my blanket, please.
I'm only playing my guitar
and looking at my tree.
But if you've nowhere else to go,
do spend some time with me."

So they sat, Bear and his visitor, talking about the snow and the wind, singing a few tunes, and enjoying Christmas Eve.

Finally, the little fellow, who was now quite warm, stood and said he really must be going.

"I thank you, Bear, for all you've done. This really has been lots of fun."

Bear stood in the doorway and watched him go off through the forest, thinking what a nice time it had been. All of a sudden his friend shouted back to him.

"Come for a ride, Bear, come with me. I'd really like your company."

A ride! On Christmas Eve! Bear grabbed his scarf and mittens and ran through the deep snow to where a big sleigh sat waiting.

The little driver turned as Bear reached the sleigh.

"Just climb up here and hang on tight. You'll be back home before it's light."

Wrapping the big quilt around him, Bear
sat down in the seat. Before he could say
"LET'S BE OFF," they were off!'

Off and up!

Up through the air and away into the snowy night. . . .

"Oh, what a Christmas!" hollered Bear.
"I've never had such fun.
I'd like to think that it could be
like this for everyone.
But most of all, just meeting you
has really brought me cheer.
Why don't we plan, my little friend,
to do this every year?"

So off they flew, far in the night and through the swirling snow, with Bear's companion laughing loud a jolly HO HO HO!

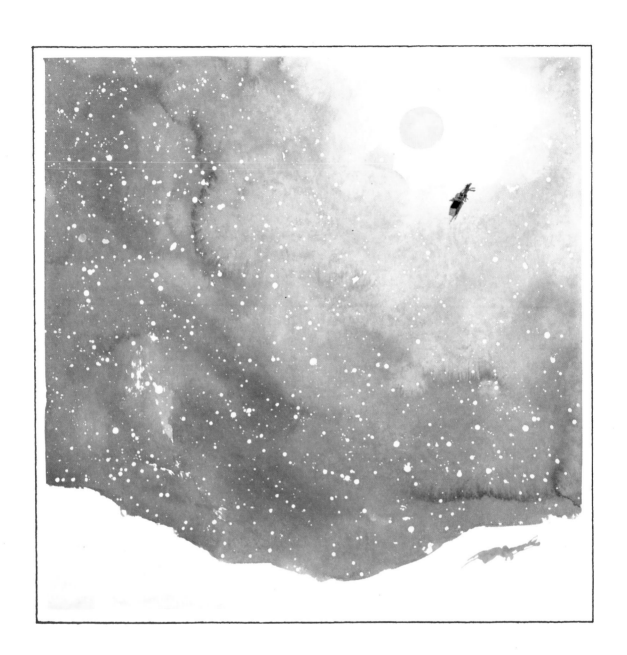